Twinkle, Twinkle, Little Bug

By Katharine Ross • Illustrated by Tom Cooke

A Random House PICTUREBACK® READER

Random House/Children's Television Workshop

"Look! A lightning bug!"
said Big Bird.

Twinkle. Twinkle. Twinkle.

Big Bird put the lightning
bug in a jar.

<u>Twinkle. Twinkle.</u>

"Look at my lightning bug,"
Big Bird said to Ernie.
"Twinkle for Ernie, little bug."
Twinkle.

"Look at my lightning bug,"
Big Bird said to Bert.
"Twinkle for Bert, little bug."
But the lightning bug
did not twinkle.

"Why won't you twinkle,
  little bug?" said Big Bird.
"Maybe he wants company,"
  said Bert.

"Twinkle for me, little bug."
Big Bird talked to
the lightning bug.
He talked and talked.
But the lightning bug
did not twinkle.

"Why won't my lightning bug twinkle?" said Big Bird. "Maybe he wants a cookie," said Cookie Monster.

Big Bird gave
the lightning bug a cookie.
But the lightning bug
still did not twinkle.

"Why won't my lightning bug
twinkle?" said Big Bird.
"Maybe he wants a leaf,"
said Oscar.

Big Bird gave the
lightning bug a leaf.

But the lightning bug
did not twinkle.

"Little bug,
  I talked to you.
  I gave you a cookie to eat.
  I gave you a leaf.
  Why won't you twinkle for me?
  I am your friend."

Big Bird set the
little bug free.
"Twinkle, little bug,"
said Big Bird.

And the lightning bug did.

<u>Twinkle. Twinkle. Twinkle.</u>

Turn the page for mini learning cards. Instructions on the inside of the back cover of this book will tell you how to use them with a child.

MINI LEARNING CARDS

See the Note to Parents on the inside back cover for ways to use the cards with your child.

a	Ernie	little	the
am	for	look	to
and	free	maybe	twinkle
at	friend	me	wants
Bert	gave	Monster	were
Big	Grover	my	why
Bird	he	not	won't
bug	I	Oscar	would
but	if	put	you
company	in	said	your
Cookie	jar	set	
did	leaf	still	
eat	lightning	talked	